THE STORY OF THE First Easter Bunny

Anthony DeStefano

Illustrated by Richard Cowdrey

SOPHIA INSTITUTE PRESS
Manchester, NH

This book is dedicated with love to my mother, Laura.
—Anthony DeStefano

Dedicated to Bob & Patty Pelfrey, who walk with Jesus.
—Richard Cowdrey

SOPHIA
INSTITUTE PRESS

Printed in the United States of America.

Sophia Institute Press®
Box 5284, Manchester, NH 03108
1-800-888-9344

www.SophiaInstitute.com

Print ISBN: 979-8-88911-100-9

Library of Congress Control Number: 2023948731

First Printing, 2023

A long time ago — over two thousand years — there lived a small bunny with very large ears.

He lived with his mother on top of a hill.
She stayed in her bed because she was ill.

Now during that time, there walked in the land
a Man who could heal with the touch of His hand.

How strange, thought the bunny. How wondrous and odd!
A Man who could heal? He must be from God!

So kissing his mother, he hopped out the door
to search for the Man, in hope of a cure.

He searched all day long, he searched high and low,
until someone told him the place he should go.

He found a large room,
just one story up,
and saw the Man praying
and lifting a cup:

"Tomorrow some soldiers will put Me to death.
I'll hang on a Cross until My last breath.
I'll lie in a tomb for three days, and then,
before the sun rises, I'll rise up again.
If you have ears, believe what I say.
Believe that I'll rise on that first Easter Day!"

The bunny was listening;
his ears opened wide.
He got so excited,
he suddenly cried:

"Yes, I have ears,
and yes, I can hear!
I believe what You say;
it's all very clear!"

He raced to get home—he practically flew.
“I must bring my mother so she can hear too!”

Back on the hill, his mom was in bed.
The rabbit leaned over, near to her head.

"Oh, Mother," he said, whispering fast,
"I've just found the Man who can cure you at last."

"I'm sorry, my son; I'm old and I'm ill.
I'm sure that I'll die in my bed on this hill."

And closing her eyes, she fell back asleep.
Her son bowed his head and started to weep.

“There’s nothing to do!” He cried all night through,
and then in the morning, he fell asleep too.

But all of a sudden, he heard a great roar.
The bunny woke up and dashed through the door.

Out in the sunlight was gathered a crowd.
The screaming and shouting were frightening and loud.

Right in the middle, a prisoner was bound.
With razor-sharp thorns His forehead was crowned.

Some men nailed His hands and His feet to a tree,
then lifted Him up for people to see.

The bunny hopped closer and looked at His face.
It seemed that he knew Him from some other place.

This prisoner hated by people so much,
was also the Man who could heal with His touch!

The bunny could see He was terribly weak.
He also could hear He was trying to speak.

He looked at His mother, His arms open wide,
and said to a friend who stood by her side:

*"This is My mother; I give her to you.
Care for her always and be her son too."*

He said to His mother: *"This is your son,"*
then gazed up to Heaven and said, *"It is done."*

As soon as He died, it started to pour.
It thundered and lightninged like never before.

The bunny stayed watching and listening until
they buried the Man on top of the hill.

A tomb in a garden was used for His grave;
they moved a large boulder to cover this cave.

The next day, the bunny
did not leave his bed.
He moaned and he groaned
and he whimpered instead.

But then he remembered
the Man had once said
that after three days
He'd rise from the dead.

Just at that moment,
he thought of a plan —
maybe *he'd* carry
his mom to the Man.

Holding her tightly,
he left their small room
and hopped out the doorway
to find the Man's tomb.

Once in the garden, he put his mom down.
She hardly was breathing and made not a sound.

By now it was evening, and no one was there.
The bunny bowed humbly and said a short prayer:

"Oh, Man in the tomb,
please won't You be kind?
You helped Your dear mother,
now won't You help mine?"

Seconds and minutes and hours went past.
The start of the day was approaching at last.

Suddenly something appeared from on high.
It came down to earth from out of the sky.

An angel of God! An angel of light!
An angel descended and lit up the night!

The angel reached forward
and touched with his hand
the stone that was blocking
the tomb of the Man.

The stone rolled away;
the tomb opened wide;
a powerful earthquake
shook the hillside.

But then something happened,
astounding to see:
out walked the Man
who had died on the tree!

The bunny was frightened and let out a sound.
The Man heard at once and looked toward the ground.

Seeing the two, He walked over where
the bunny was tending his mother with care.

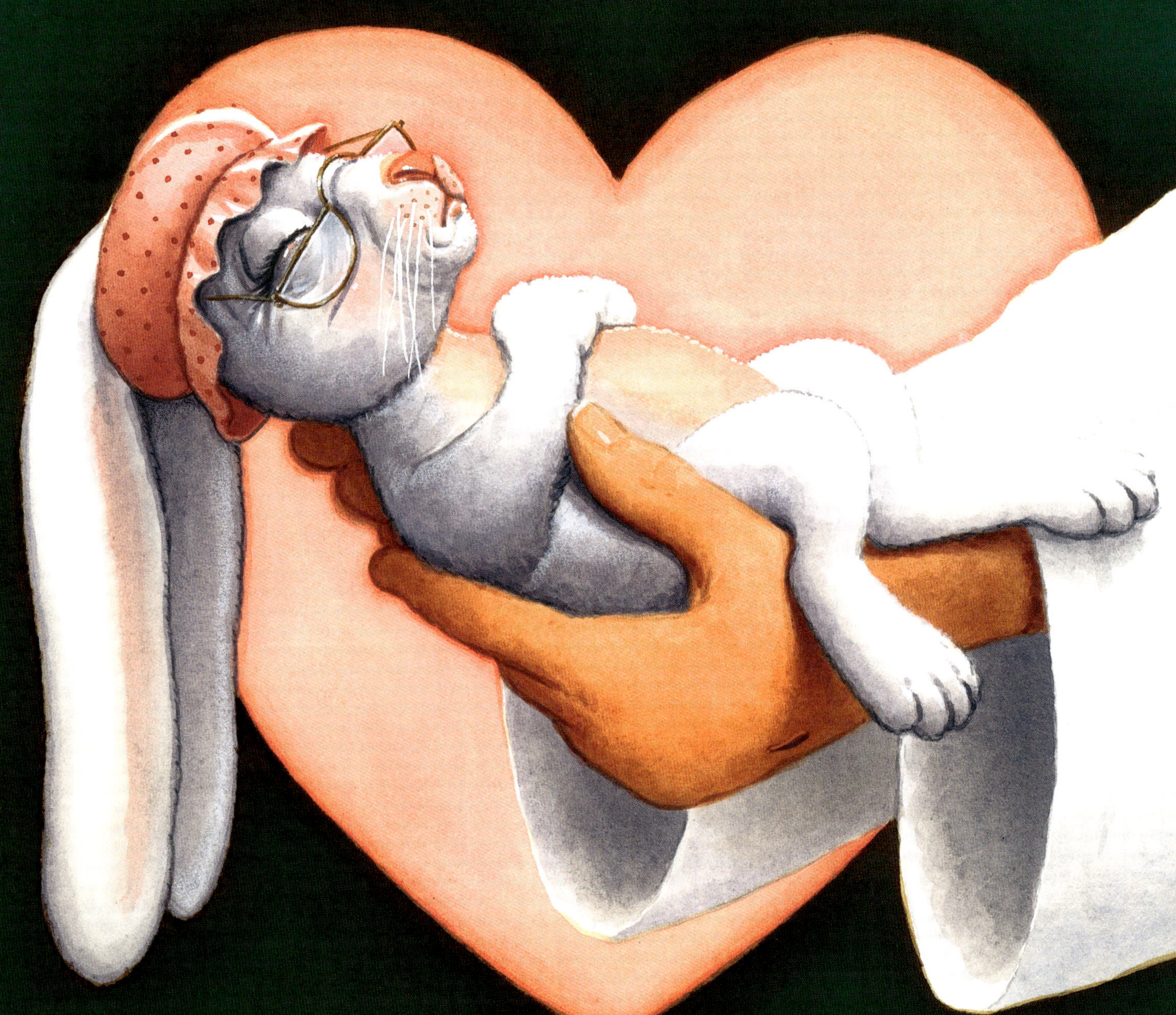

He looked at the mother and bent down to her;
He picked her up gently and petted her fur.

Laying her back, the Man turned to go;
the sun was just rising, His face was aglow.

The bunny turned ’round,
and to his surprise,
his mother had risen
and opened her eyes.

His mom was awake!
His mom was awake!
His heart was so happy,
he thought it would break!

The Man who had healed her
was walking away;
the two watched together
and knelt down to pray.

And so ever after,
the bunny would say,
the Man saved his mother
that first Easter Day.

He started to tell
everyone that he knew,
the Man had the power
to save THEIR lives too!

And many were saved
because they believed
the life-changing news
that they had received.

Because of his passionate faith in the Man,
the fame of the bunny spread through the land.

That's why we've remembered — for two thousand years —
this small Easter Bunny with very large ears.